Lantern

Burgundy Athena Pendragon

Cover Art by Aaron Joseph

Illustrations by Aaron Joseph

Design and Formatting by Shaii Jaff

Author Portrait by jem zero

ISBN: 978-1-961603-00-4

Library of Congress Control Number: 2023911856

First edition: 2023

Bull & Dragon Press LLC.

All books and works by Burgundy Athena Pendragon can be found at BurgundyPendragon.gay

For information about upcoming releases, information can also be found at BullAndDragonPress.com

6808 University Ave Ste 108
Middleton, WI 53562-2779
USA

For Mom, for always believing in me and supporting me when it felt like no one else did, for fighting a battle of chronic illness and being one of the toughest nuts I know.

For my grandmother, who wanted to die on her own terms, and who was not granted that freedom by those around her.

And for my friends and strangers who are fighting battles that few others can understand. May you find joy through the darkness.

Dear Readers,

This book contains depictions of blood, murder, death, mental illness, terminal enchantment, body morphing, and suicidal ideation.

If any of these topics are not to your liking, then please, I promise not to be offended that you have chosen to set this down and read something else.

LINDWORM'S
FIRE

Lantern

"What do you want?" Devyn asked the woman in front of zir. "Haven't seen you in years."

"I'm here to collect on that favor you owe me," she said. Her name was Akácia, an old friend of zirs. She and Devyn sat across from each other at a table at the *Lindworm's Fire*, an exorcist and assorted light mage guild for the backcountry of the central region.

Devyn leaned back in zir seat, gripping tightly the square glass lantern in zir hand.

"Fantastic. You barely write and never send telegrams, suddenly you show up and you're not even here to catch up and say 'hi' or grab a drink?"

"Sorry, dear, I've had a lot going on since the last time we were together." She glanced at Devyn's lantern cautiously. "You keeping her contained?"

"Sure am," zie patted the lantern. "The power of subjugation. Now, what do I owe you?"

"Never did like dark magic. Anyways, my son got cursed by this medallion he looted on his last quest—"

"—Well that was his *first* mistake," Devyn rolled zir eyes. "Don't steal random artifacts, and don't go on quests."

"It was from a dragon horde!"

"That's even worse! Dragons are immune to human curses!"

"*Anyways*, he needs to get his curse lifted but doesn't know how. We've tried healers of all types and none of them have been able to help."

"Right. What's the curse entail? Or the medallion?"

"He turns into a horrible beast every half-moon."

"Half-moon? What type of beast? Serpent? Wolf? Cat? Bear? Sounds like a weird strain of lycanthropy."

"I…I'm not sure, actually. You'd have to see it for yourself, but it's not lycanthropy, we've tried that already. It's not vampirism either."

Intrigued, Devyn shifted forward to meet Akácia's gaze. Zie stared through her as she gave zir an expression Devyn recognized to be desperation. Tears welled in the corners of her brown eyes.

"Please," she pleaded, "you're the only one who can help him. He's suffering. It only gets worse with each change. I just want him to stop suffering from this curse. You're his last hope."

Zie extended a hand to her.

"I'll do whatever I can to help. I promise."

◗

Devyn wasn't entirely sure why Akácia thought zie was the best one suited for the job. Zie had been an exorcist for twenty-five years, a specialization in the broader field of light magic. The two had been light mage apprentices together with Kinai—*Kinai*. Zie clenched the lantern's handle. *I'm sorry, friend.*

The demonic lantern glowed in the darkness of the forest, illuminating Devyn's green-cloaked hooded figure as zie made zir way to a distant village. Taking a carriage only took zir part of the way to the residence of Akácia's son, Lio. He'd been moved to the monk temple far away from major civilization, she'd explained to Devyn.

"It's to keep him away from town, but also the monks know prayer magic, they might know something the others didn't."

"I don't see how monks will do any better than the healers you went to," Devyn had grumbled, "but at least healing *works*."

Annoyed, Akácia had shot back, "at least they're trying! If healing magic isn't helping him, then prayer magic might!"

"Prayer magic doesn't *do* anything. They should be leaving this curse-breaking nonsense to the experts. All they're gonna do is make Lio feel like a lost cause."

She had sighed, "may the Holy Mother be with you."

"And with you," Devyn had said mechanically.

Zie approached a wooden two-story temple in the woods with steep eaves and a horned ornament. Lights flickered on inside. Zir own lantern flickered excitedly.

Deep inside zir mind, the lantern's voice said, *"I'm hungry. Feed me, damn it!"*

"Yes, yes, I know. I'll feed you soon. Be patient."

Devyn approached the temple and knocked.

A tall monk in indigo robes answered the door.

"Ah, you must be the exorcist friend that Akácia hired."

"That's correct. My name is Devyn Torez," zie bowed.

"Excellent," the monk bowed, "we're glad you made it here safely so late at night. Come inside."

Devyn got one foot in the doorway, only to be stopped at the lantern by a light magic barrier.

"My friend, I must apologize, *dark magic* and *demons* are not normally permitted inside the temple," the monk explained.

"I understand that," Devyn said, "but Jackie is under my control. She won't hurt anyone." *Unless I order her to.* "Besides, for best results she needs to be near me at all times, or I may lose my grip on her."

That was only partly true. Subjugation magic was largely a battle of wills, one's spirit had to be unbendable, unyielding to the other *at the time* of subjugation. After that the deed was done, and as long as the enchantment remained intact and the object of containment unbroken, Jackie the primeval fire spirit would be magically bound to Devyn Torez as a magical demonic slave. Zie counted on the monk not being intimately familiar with the intricacies of dark magic. Admitting that zie was cautiously anxious about losing Jackie if zie left her out of zir sight for too long was not a fact that would go over well.

The monk looked from Jackie the Lantern to Devyn.

Zie added slowly, "I don't think a rampaging fire spirit is something any of us want to deal with."

The monk's eyes widened, "no, no it isn't."

"If the Head Monk has a problem, I'll explain the situation to him," zie assured.

"Jackie, you may enter, too," the monk said.

The inside of the temple was largely bare, with a finely made rug in the center and intricate tapestries along the walls. There was a low table along the back wall.

"Here are your quarters," he said. Then he left. Devyn set zir stuff down.

"*I'm hungry!*" Jackie complained.

"Alright, alright, I am, too," Devyn said. Zie picked her up and they left the temple to hunt.

"*Don't the monks have food?*"

"Probably, but it's much less rude to hunt."

"*I suppose.*"

Devyn sat patiently under a tree outside the line of sight of the temple, waiting, meditating with the lantern between zir legs.

Crickets chirped. Jackie's light made it easy to find them. Devyn concentrated, focusing zir will over the crickets. Silent magic, just like subjugation, required immense concentration. Magical chains materialized and wrapped the small animals. Caught, Devyn casually picked them up and opened the lantern a small amount. A gaping fiery mouth enveloped the crickets.

The lantern burped.

If given the opportunity, she would devour Devyn without hesitation.

◑

"What're we trying this time?" Lio asked zir.

Devyn was running preliminary tests, a magical second opinion, so to speak.

"Testing for ogreism this time. It's curse only. Many mistake it for lycanthropy, which is just treatable, but ogreism is curable—with the right parts." Devyn was reasonably optimistic about Lio's case. Zir paid profession was exorcism, a subsect of zir mastering light magic, but after the five years of light magic training were over, Devyn had taken it upon zirself to study dark magic and in the process discovered the interdisciplinary field of monster magic. At twenty-five years of experience in magic wielding, zie was one of the best in the land and one of but a single handful who practiced monster magic. While Devyn did not have hundreds of ingredient combinations memorized like a trained healing specialist would, zie had zir *Big Book of Monster Magic*, a living document of an encyclopedia of anything that zie or a future person would need to know related to monster magic. It saved zir a lot of trouble memorizing information—because spouting situational spells and incantations in structured rhyme was enough of a pain!

Zie had zir *Big Book of Monster Magic* out on the temple floor, salt circle mandala around Lio, with precise incense and enchanted beads, dried onions, and mead. Devyn chanted a specific song from the book.

The onions burned up.

Devyn and Lio coughed.

"Shoot," Devyn wheezed, "it's not ogreism." If it had

been, the mead would've disappeared. The onions were put in place so Devyn knew if the ritual had been done correctly or not. Not standard practice. Onions stunk so the practice of decoys didn't catch on, but Devyn liked knowing that no reaction meant the ritual had been done improperly.

Lio and Devyn reeked of burnt onions. Zie tried two vampirism tests, five different lycanthropy tests, trollism, and searched every curse and enchanted artifact within the *Big Book of Monster Magic*. Many of the entries were added by Devyn, the pages covered in notes from the past couple decades.

Lio sighed, "no one knows what's wrong with me." He was young, fifteen years old, thin, wiry, and his whole life ahead of him.

"I know, but I'm going to help," Devyn said. The stolen artifact was inside a golden box with a warning label that'd been placed there by another healer. "You're going to be fine." *I told Akácia that I would do this. I can't fail her.*

Devyn's second night at the temple was also the half-moon. The monks brought a willing Lio down to the dedicated were-den in the basement. Chained with silver to the wall behind steel bars, Lio looked pathetic. This was standard procedure.

The monks formed a prayer chain outside the cage, candles glowing in-between each person. They roped Devyn into participating. Zie grumbled inwardly but wasn't going to be rude. It was to help alleviate Lio's suffering. The sentiment was sweet, but as Lio morphed into a creature barely recognizable as human, a demon with the scales and fangs of a dragon, the body of an ogre, the face of a rhinoceros, the eyes of a catamount, the ears of an ass, and the distorted voice of Lio, he shrieked in pain as his body transformed. Devyn's heart lurched, remembering the cries of Kinai. They screamed the same.

The night was long. At an interval between prayers, Devyn had to step out, taking zir lantern with zir. She was Devyn's burden to bear, not the monks'.

"I've never seen anything like that, and I'm ancient!"

"You said it, not me," Devyn said. "That medallion he stole is something else." Zie forced the memory of Kinai's death to the back of zir mind. Jackie was the *last* being to talk to about it. In fact, there was no one to talk to. Akácia was never around for the same reason zie couldn't talk to Jackie. Zie chose not to attach to many people, for an exorcist who also dealt with monster magic led a dangerous life, but someone had to do it. Even experts made mistakes or fell victim to underestimation or slip-ups or faltering hearts, as the untimely fate of Kinai demonstrated.

"Any idea what it is?" She asked casually. It's not like she had anything else to do.

"Unfortunately, no. And I'm not overly acquainted with enchanted artifacts. That's someone else's job."

"You might be able to ask the dragon he stole it from if they know anything about it."

"Hmmmm… that's not a bad idea. I'll see what the monks know tomorrow." With that, Devyn returned to the were-den and helped the monks with their prayer. Zie didn't think it helped.

Lio returned to normal when the sunrise trickled into the basement. The Head Monk took Lio back to his room. Devyn spent the morning writing a new entry in the *Big Book of Monster Magic*.

●

Devyn finished an exorcism of the temple, as a courtesy for the hospitality. Several spirits fled the grounds, looking to be harmless enough. Jackie was left outside—zie didn't want to deal with *that* inevitable disaster. Zie and Lio then went into town to see what the library had on enchanted artifacts. As it turned out, the monks donated their books on that to the public, so questers would stop pestering them.

Lio was a cheerful young man, friendly with the locals. A little too friendly, in Devyn's opinion, because he liked to talk openly about his curse to people inquiring about their research.

"Lio quit flirting," zie scolded, "the sooner we find what we're looking for, the sooner we can find out what's wrong with you, and the sooner I can help."

"You're already helping!" he said.

"I haven't done a thing to help," Devyn growled. "Nothing any of us has done has been any help at all."

"You're trying!" Lio protested. "That counts for something!" They perused the magic books. They found three relevant books: *Enchanted Artifacts and Cursed Treasure in the Central Region*; *Notable Sorcerers, Witches, and Mages*; and *Dark Magic Users of the Central Region*. Lio took on the *Enchanted Artifacts* book, Devyn scoured the two history books.

"How? You're still dealing with this unknown curse, you're still suffering, and we don't know what it is." Zie scanned through a section on summoners. Jackie was on the counter.

"I mean, I guess if you put it *that* way, but I think that's really cynical, and it means a lot to me that you and the monks are making such an effort to help me." Lio beamed at zir.

Devyn rolled zir eyes. "Don't misunderstand me. I'm only here to make good on a *huge* favor that I owe your mother."

Lio snorted, "I know. I still appreciate it."

"His optimism is annoying—can I eat him!? I'm sick of his stupid face!"

Devyn growled at her, "cut that out. You *know* I *hate* that."

"What're you gonna do? Kill me?"

"Only when I die," zie assured, "but in the meantime, have some water." Devyn trapped a couple water droplets into the lantern. Zir skin burned.

Jackie cursed many expletives.

Lio stared at the interaction, confused.

"Who're you talking to?" he asked.

Devyn pointed to Jackie. "Her. I have a fire spirit bound to that lantern."

Lio nodded, "oh. Doesn't that hurt her?"

"That's the point," Devyn said, scanning the next page within zir book.

"That's kinda mean," Lio said.

"Yes, it is!" Jackie agreed. **"Big jerkface!"**

"That's the point," Devyn said sternly. "It won't kill her, just keep her in line."

Lio didn't say anything else. They read in silence, save for Jackie's commentary on whatever Devyn was reading.

Devyn and Lio trekked through the twilight forest toward the werewolf pack. Another half-moon had passed, and just as Akácia had said, Lio's transformation did get worse. For now, the monks could comfort him in his monstrous state, and human Lio could recall it and express gratitude; but he thrashed around more aggressively, and he cried more at the transformations. Their research at the library came up with nothing.

The full moon was tomorrow, and Devyn hoped to make acquaintance with the werewolves so that they would be willing to impart their knowledge at the next half-moon. Zie purposely told Lio to come unarmed, so between the two of them Jackie was their only weapon. She was *Devyn's* only weapon. People always underestimated the unarmed stranger with the lantern.

They walked through the night. In all honesty, Devyn had no idea where the werewolves lived, but trespassing on their territory at night was a good way to ensure interacting with them.

Sure enough, an hour until dawn, a trio of humans with knives and a bow approached them. Two women and a man.

"Who goes there?" The short-haired woman asked. "State your purpose!"

"Good morning!" Devyn said. "My name is Devyn. This is Lio. We're looking for the werewolves?"

"Who sent you?" The male asked, holding out his dagger.

Lio chimed in, "we're looking for the alpha werewolf!"

The werewolves rolled their eyes.

Devyn smacked him.

"Ow! What was that for?" Lio asked, rubbing his arm.

"There's no such thing as alpha and beta wolves," Devyn said.

The long-haired lady werewolf said, "yeah, it's actually a misnomer, and it horribly misrepresents the nature of wolf and werewolf society."

Lio was about to say something, but he stopped himself.

The werewolves gave them a look-see, a pat-down, a weapons check, and a sniff check.

"Clear!" said the short-haired lady werewolf. "I suppose we can take you to the pack. You seem alright—Devyn, was it? I suggest your friend shuts up if you want the elder to take you seriously."

The werewolf patrol guided Devyn and Lio the rest of the way, a half-hour of listening to the three bicker and banter. It reminded Devyn of zir apprenticeship days with Akácia and Kinai all those years ago: the laughs, the struggles, the mischief, and... before they became exorcists, before that fateful day. Zie clenched the lantern tighter, anger and sorrow intumescing in zir heart.

At the edge of the forest was a field of tall grasses billowing in the breeze. A pack of human werewolves, twenty or thirty, was set-up at the outskirts of the clearing with a singular, substantial, tent-like structure that easily housed the entirety of the werewolf pack.

Lio whispered to Devyn, "they live in a *tent?* What are they, *wolves?*" The grin told Devyn that he was attempting humor.

"That's not funny. Your mother would be ashamed of you for saying that."

"Ouch. I thought I was the one made of fire here!"

"You're no fun," he rolled his eyes.

"That attitude of yours is exactly what got you cursed in the first place," Devyn said flatly.

"How!?"

"Carelessness and not thinking before you act." *Akácia, he's lucky I care about you. And I owe you.*

The sun rose and the residents stirred. Their guides entered the building through a deerskin flap, then emerged a few minutes later with an elderly person, helping them balance.

Devyn bowed to the elder. Lio clumsily mimicked.

"Good morning, you must be the ones the patrol told me about. You're here to speak with me, yes?"

"Yes, Your Honor, my name is Devyn Torez. I'm an exorcist of twenty-years' experience, plus five years of light magic apprenticeship. And this is Lio, my patient."

"Pleasure to meet you."

"I've come to you this morning seeking your wisdom and experience, and to show good faith I have brought with us the ingredients for lycanthropy treatment—should anyone in your pack want it."

The elder nodded approvingly. "This is an excellent gift. Thank you. Let us talk inside."

Inside the semi-permanent hide-clad building was a firepit with coals, dozens of animal hide blankets, and metal utensils, kitchenware, and assorted tools. There was also a stack of books far away from the fire. People stirred as the sunlight woke them up.

Lio was given time to explain his story, how he and his friend had gone on a quest that sent them to a dragon's horde, and Lio laid claim to a medallion in a gold chest that he put around his neck. His companion touched it too but was unaffected by the half-moon curse. He talked about the three other exorcists and healers Akácia had taken him to see, and how each of them came up with nothing, how she'd reached out to an old friend of her and his father's as a last resort.

"Not even Devyn knows what's wrong," he said. "And my transformations hurt more and more, and it's getting harder and harder to control myself, or recognize who people are."

The elder listened intently to everything.

Devyn said, "and this is why I have sought you out, Your Honor. I have tried everything and consulted all of the materials at my disposal, and I know nothing except what he *doesn't* have." Zie pulled out a detailed drawing of the medallion. It had been left at the temple for the safety of any strangers they came across.

The elder examined the drawing.

"Hmmm… I'm sorry, this artifact doesn't ring a bell." As the elder spoke, Devyn carefully set to work preparing the ingredients, turning them into the treatment medicine in front of the recipients. It was good practice and established trust with werefolks, so they knew the medicine wasn't poisoned by malicious sorts who thought they deserved to die. It was an inconvenience, sure, but Devyn didn't complain. The medicine had to be prepared somewhere at some time, and if doing it in front of werefolks was a show of benign intentions, then so be it. Werewolves were ostracized by the unenchanted, few willing to find it in their hearts to understand the chronic suffering of the enchanted, or help them alleviate their pain or their cursed urges. In twenty-five years of magehood, Devyn had met but a small handful of werefolks, vampires, and others who—under sound mind—genuinely wanted to spread their curses or hurt anyone. Yet few healers wanted to listen or help werefolks and other enchanted types. They were monsters to be slain, not humans to be helped.

And now Lio was one of them, too. Sure, he'd been careless and foolish, but rarely did someone deserve such a fate. After his earlier scolding Lio had been largely quiet, aside from recounting his own story. Zie could only hope the best of him.

The elder was slow to recall, but a couple hours into their meeting the elder finally said, "I remember, when I was a child, there was a woman who had been cursed with an untreatable enchantment who lived with our pack. She turned twice a month, always when we weren't, so we would stay up all night with her as we do for all our packmates. The transformation started off fine, but overtime it became unbearable for her. With no hope for a better future, she drove a silver dagger into her heart."

Devyn processed that. Lio flinched.

"Thank you for sharing," Devyn said. "I very much appreciate you telling us that."

"Of course. If you visit again before moonrise on the next half-moon, I'd be able to tell you for sure if your friend here is the same creature."

As additional goodwill toward the werewolves, Devyn went through the rituals to find out which strains of lycanthropy a couple of the newer members had, which was determined by exorcist magic. Zie wrote down the exact ratios of the five strains within the pack. Unfortunately, Devyn hadn't brought ingredients for Type D because it and Type E (what the elder and their descendants had) weren't very common, and all five strains were present in the pack.

"It is almost sundown," the elder warned. "It will be unsafe for you here."

Devyn shrugged, "we'll be fine." Lio balked at zir.

"Are you nuts!?" He asked.

"The most virulent and aggressive ones have been given medication for the evening. There's nothing to worry about," Devyn assured. "And if not, we'll still be fine."

Lio hesitated, then said, "okay, if you say so."

The evening rituals began.

The Type A werewolves –the ones with no pain but turned into violent monsters trying to bite every human they came across—were chained to trees using silver chains. Medication gave them control of themselves. The Type E werewolves—entirely composed of the elder, their daughter, and two grandchildren—were the only ones not chained. They would only become mindless, in pain, and violent during an eclipse, but otherwise it was passed down through the bloodline, as was Type C. Amongst the pack were seven children of various ages, only three of them hereditary. The other four Devyn tested: one was Type A and three were Type B.

Devyn chose to stay for two reasons: first, it was another show of good faith and establishment of trust by staying to make sure the medication worked, and second, to teach Lio a lesson he needed to learn.

As the sun set and the transformations began, the unmedicated shrieked in pain and agony, their bodies turning against them as they did every full moon.

The worst were the children.

Not even Jackie said anything. It was horrible to listen to.

Lio visibly winced, plugging his ears.

The transformations finished. Lio sat there stunned.

Immediately, the chained ones were checked. The medication worked, so the Type A, B, and C werewolves were unchained by Devyn, the elder, and the other three. No one wanted to be chained down any more than any of them wanted to chain their friends down, but without proper medical care there was no other viable option to keep them from hurting themselves and others.

The pack was happy to be together and free, but rather than run off into the wilderness they stayed by their howling and struggling Type D friends.

Lio said softly to Devyn, "may the Holy Mother have mercy on them."

Devyn grunted.

"What?" he asked.

"Don't worry about it." The children's cries rang in Devyn's ears.

There was a long silence, until finally Lio asked, "who is she, Devyn?"

"She's a primeval fire spirit," zie said.

"Primeval spirit? Aren't those the beings we're told about as children?"

"Who walked the world before humans crawled out of the mud? Yes, the same."

"How——?"

"Sometimes they wake up from their long sleeps. Some are benign, some wreak havoc, some you don't even notice. Jackie wreaked havoc."

"This time! Sometimes I don't."

"Is…" Lio started to ask. Devyn had a good guess what he was trying to ask. "Is she the one who killed my dad?"

Slowly, Devyn nodded. "Yes. She murdered Kinai. And hundreds of others."

"Why do you keep her with you?"

"Because I'm the only one who can."

"Why not kill her?"

"This will kill her. It's the only way."

"I… I don't understand. What happened that day? Mom refuses to talk about it."

"Akácia—your mother, has her reasons. But she's not here right now." She was away on an exorcism mission. "So, I'll tell you. You deserve to know what happened to your father."

The elder werewolf moseyed over to them.

"Pardon my intrusion. I'm a nosey old dog and I heard talk about the primevals," the elder said.

"By all means. I don't mind. Stories like this should be shared to those who seek the knowledge," Devyn said. "Lio, are you fine with it?"

He nodded.

"It was ten years ago. Akácia, Kinai, and I were summoned by the Grand Council, along with dozens of other exorcists across the country, on a call that a malevolent primeval spirit had woken from her slumber and was terrorizing villages."

"That sounds familiar," the elder mused. "We were advised to stay near water."

"The historians told us that it was Jakevais the Fire Elemental, who would wake up every few thousand years, usually to cause chaos. From sporadic wildfires to burning villages to devouring people whole to less violent tomfoolery. We were prepped on what to expect based on the last time she awoke, and the plan was to put her to sleep. Past exorcists did the same with a wind spirit every century. But Jakevais was different. She could and would burn humans who opposed her, devouring them. She was a challenge that no one knew how to counter or protect against, except water magic but even then, that couldn't kill her. She couldn't be killed unless she was bound to a mortal body. No one wanted to attempt it. The conjoining ceremony had only been successfully achieved once and with a water spirit. Finding someone with the willpower to stand against Jakevais would be a feat in of itself, but before doing that we had to subdue her. *Either way*, we had to subdue her. The Grand Council told us to put her to sleep and in another hundred years we'd deal with her again, and again, and again, and again. So, we teamed up with the water mages. There was thirty of us in all, fifteen exorcists and fifteen water mages. Your parents and I were on the task force together."

"They left me with my grandparents," Lio said. "I never saw dad again."

"I remember. I was there when we dropped you off."

"That's right! You were!" Lio lit up at the memory.

"The plan went well for about ten minutes. We had Jakevais cornered, but we underestimated her tolerance for water, and she broke through our offenses. Several of us were killed in our battle with her. We struggled to subdue her, and we lost numbers, making it harder to put her to sleep. So, in a last-ditch effort, Kinai and I saw an opportunity to bind Jakevais's soul to ours. As she was distracted, we performed the ritual—" Devyn held out zir right palm, displaying the blade scar. "But the ceremony requires your will to be unbending, unyielding, uncorruptible. When Jakevais lashed out at Akácia, he faltered, he hesitated. I felt him second-guess the plan, and he broke concentration in order to help Akácia, and his soul perished. But I didn't. My resolve did not falter."

"Wait, you were just going to let mom die!?" Lio asked.

"Yes." Devyn heard Jackie snort a laugh. Zie ignored her.

"Why!?"

"It's not like I *wanted* her to die. The ceremony requires you to be unbending and uncorruptible. The lives of future generations were more important than the life of one friend, no matter how much she means to me. Besides, she *lived*. In fact, only five of us lived. The other three were water mages."

"Maybe that's why mom doesn't see you much."

"Pretty certain it's because I have your father's murderer kept in a lantern and I call her Jackie."

"…oh." Lio paused for a moment. "I—hmmm…"

"Speak your mind."

"I'm having a hard time understanding why you use dark magic, when you clearly care a lot about others."

"Dark magic isn't necessarily evil. I'm a human just using the tools of the world at my disposal to try doing what's right."

"I don't understand how you use dark magic for good."

"Sometimes it's the only tool available."

After being up for well over a day, they returned to the temple in silence, save for Jackie rambling about a werecat lover she had a few thousand years ago. Devyn spent the walk in deep thought, thinking about Akácia, Kinai, and their son's condition.

Akácia, why did you ask me? I hadn't seen you in ten years. You rarely write. I know you're busy, and I know it's hard for you to be around me. I understand all of that. But why ask me? You've given me what feels like an impossible task. Why would you entrust me with you and Kinai's son?

With little lead on Lio's curse, Devyn had to do business around town to bring in an income. There weren't many exorcists in the area, so Devyn had a steady stream of clients. Lio would tag along out of boredom, or because he wanted company other than the monks. Twice there were clients who wanted an exorcism done, purification rituals, but when zie saw that they wanted their mentally ill or *different* family member to be purified, Devyn refused the job both times.

"There's nothing wrong with her," Devyn told zir clients. "Demons aren't possessing her, she's just different."

"Can't you purify her anyways? She must be a changeling! That isn't the child I gave birth to!"

Devyn sighed in annoyance. "Ma'am, I can *personally* assure you that she's not a changeling, she's not possessed, and I'm not going to do something that I *know* for sure will do nothing."

"You're a quack!"

"Have a good day, ma'am."

The townsfolk became increasingly aware of Devyn's

real reason for being there, but only because Lio couldn't keep his trap shut!

"What're you getting so upset for?" Lio asked, rolling his eyes. "There's no harm. No one seems to mind that I have a curse."

"That's because you haven't transformed in front of them. Being enchanted is fine for some, until you present its symptoms."

The first real conflict they had with anyone was a band of ruffians while they were out gathering supplies from the wilderness. Devyn was doing a spore check on a fairy ring mushroom, so they'd set up camp for the day to collect other supplies while the cap sat under a glass jar on a piece of paper, waiting for the moisture to gather.

Then the bandits showed up.

"How rude," Jackie said. ***"We were having a nice day. Can I eat them!?"***

"Evening," Devyn said. Lio had his dagger drawn. "What can we do for you?"

"You can give us your stuff," a bandit said. "And your money."

"What makes you think I have anything of value?" zie asked.

"We know who you are, we know you have money." Five blades pointed at them from all sides.

"Lemme take them," Lio whispered.

Devyn whispered back, "hold your horses. I've got this." Zie said to the bandits, "I really don't think that's a good idea. Is there anything you'd like instead? Help? Do you have a demon problem?"

"Quit talking or we'll cut you," another bandit said.

"I *really* think you should reconsider your actions."

"Shut up and do as we say!"

So much for diplomacy. Lantern in hand, Devyn commanded firmly, "fire."

Flames erupted from the lantern, encircling zir hand and bursting forth like a flamethrower. Zie directed the flamethrower at the bandits, and they jumped back. One threw a knife at zir.

"Shield."

A protective barrier of white magic materialized, blocking the blade. It fell to the ground. Devyn aimed the flamethrower at the nearest bandit, who ran away with their tail between their legs.

With the ruffians gone, Lio exclaimed, "holy cow! Devyn, that was amazing! How did you do that?"

Devyn put the fire out with another command, "finish." A bit confused by the question, Devyn said, "Lio, I literally trained in light magic for five years with your parents. I don't know what you're so surprised about."

He blushed. "You just always act all grumpy and you've got your leaves and your onions…"

Devyn snorted, "I guess that's fair."

◐

The next half-moon was tonight.

Devyn took Lio to see the werewolves again, this

time with a proper supply of ingredients to match the specific needs of the pack, including the elder's family. Lio seemed antsy.

"Are you sure this is a good idea?" Lio asked.

"I'm sure. I won't let you hurt anyone, or yourself."

Again, they ran into a patrol, and they were guided to the pack. This time the patrol was expecting them. At the werewolf commune the elder greeted them, and Devyn set to work on the medicine while Lio talked with the werewolves. It was their turn to watch the spectacle.

The sun was setting. Lio sat in the middle of the field. Devyn sat with him.

He was crying.

"Devyn, I don't want to do this!" He shook.

Zie held him. "Ssshhhh… I know. I know it hurts. It'll be over soon."

The last rays of sunlight disappeared behind the horizon. Lio's body convulsed and swelled and morphed into the dragon-hide horned beast. Devyn released zir hug, stepping back to give Lio space.

He cried out in pain, his screams becoming monstrous roars.

The human werewolves watched from the treeline.

"Lio! Can you hear me!?" Devyn called out to him.

Roaring.

The transformation finished. Monster Lio stood still in the field, breathing heavily. He stepped forward to examine Devyn.

No recognition.

Devyn allowed Monster Lio to walk around and explore, on guard and ready to subdue. For now, he wasn't doing anything wrong.

Zie sat in the grass that night. Most of the werewolves went to bed, the scene safe and the spectacle over—except the elder, who joined zir in the grass.

"Is this the same beast you saw all those years ago?" zie asked.

The elder nodded, "I'm afraid so."

Devyn sighed, "I was afraid you'd say that."

"What're you going to do?"

"I… I don't know. But we haven't tried everything. There's gotta be something."

When Lio returned to normal, he woke in a daze, tears staining his face. They bid the elder a good morning and left.

An hour of silence passed before Lio finally said, "I can't remember anything."

"Not even me talking to you?"

"No. Just pain."

This was the first time he couldn't remember the night.

He asked, "so… what's the verdict from the elder?"

"The elder says you match the appearance."

"What does that mean? This is going to continue to get worse until I become a violent, uncontrollable monster?"

"… I—I don't know. But, yes, that's what it sounds

like."

"Devyn?"

"Yes?"

"I want my mom."

●

Devyn was writing to Akácia a couple days later, updating her on what had happened, when the Head Monk knocked on zir door.

"I need to talk to you about Lio."

"Come in. If it's about the herb stores I used on him, I promise I'll have the restock prepared by tomorrow—"

"What?" the Head Monk said. "No, no, that's fine."

"Then…?"

"It's his mental state."

"What of it?"

"He's been asking the other monks some concerning questions."

Could you be less vague? Zie thought. Out loud, zie said, "such as?"

"You know what I'm talking about."

"*No*, I don't," Devyn said firmly, "so I'd really appreciate it if you didn't talk to me as if I can read your mind, and you dropped the ambiguities."

"Right. My apologies. Lio's been asking about mortality, the meaning of life, death…"

"And why is this concerning?"

"I'm concerned that he may be considering suicide."

Devyn's heart tightened. "I don't blame him."

"Devyn! That's blasphemy! The Holy Mother frowns upon suicide, he'll never be allowed to reincarnate, she'll turn his soul into a demon—or worse, destroy him!"

I really don't think she cares that much. Devyn didn't argue with the Head Monk. "What do you want me to do about it?"

"I want you to talk to him, and talk him out of it."

Devyn bit zir tongue. "Why can't you do it?"

"He listens to you. You *can't* let him kill himself. He's got a full life ahead of him. His suicide would be a stain on the sanctity of this temple, and the Holy Mother will be displeased with all of us if we allow him to throw his life away: the gift of life that she's *blessed* him with!"

Devyn forced out a polite, "okay. I'll talk to him."

☽

Devyn and Lio packed several days' worth of clothes and food, water was limited, and they brought Devyn's *Big Book of Monster Magic*. They were going on a long trip to the dragon cave that Lio had stolen from several moons ago.

As had been firmly demanded of zir, Devyn spoke with Lio about his research.

"Look, I understand your feelings," Devyn had said, "and to be completely honest, I think they're justified. But the Head Monk he is uh…"

"Making you talk to me about it?"

"I would've said he *strongly suggested* it, but yes."

"Don't worry, I overheard. Temple walls aren't very thick."

"How do you feel?"

"I'm not sure… I-I don't really get why it's such a big deal… he talked to me and he made me feel so *bad* about it that now I… I guess I won't. But I don't know what kind of life he thinks I'm going to lead."

"You *can* lead a long and fulfilling life, even with this curse. Werefolks can have amazing lives."

"Sure, and I know I'd be restrained every two weeks, but it's just going to get worse until I start becoming violent, too, and—and what if I hurt someone?"

Devyn had noticed that in every cycle it seemed that Lio had been struggling under the chains defensively, a sharp contrast to their visit to the werewolves. Those chains wouldn't hold him forever. They weren't designed for him.

Lio looked dejected. "Other werefolks have medicine they can take. No medicine has worked on me."

Devyn felt zir heart clench in guilt. New medicines could only be tested every other week, and zie had now tried nine, all painkillers that worked on enchantments. Nothing zie did helped. Nothing.

The journey to the dragon cave took them far to the north, a month-long journey they mostly took by carriage along the main roads. When they returned Akácia would hopefully be waiting for them at the temple, back from her mission two-hundred miles away.

Devyn and Lio finally arrived in a fortress-like city covered in a fresh layer of snow. The gate was guarded by a pair of golems, who let them into the city after asking a few questions.

Considering the season, Devyn asked around about the dragon at the local guild and at the library, which got confused looks from the patrons.

"Dragon?" One guild woman said. "Ain't got one of those, but we do got a lindworm up yonder. That might be what you're looking for."

Devyn spun around, glowering at Lio.

"A *lindworm!?* You told me it was a *dragon!*"

Lio shrugged, "close enough. What's the difference?"

Appalled, Devyn exclaimed, "what's the dif——? No! They are *not* the same thing! Completely different orders, completely different magic, different social norms—I thought they were extinct here! Gaw! I'm prepared to talk to a dragon, not a lindworm!"

Devyn went into a frenzied panic, too stressed to explain the problem to him.

Zie spent the evening stressing over what gift they were going to bring, and more importantly, how they were going to speak to the lindworm!

"Too many syllables," Jackie said as Devyn practiced zir poetic speech. ***"I don't understand why you're messing this up. This should be nothing to you."*** All advanced magic was performed with rhyming, situational, incantations that fit into twenty-syllable stanzas. Half of magic training was spent just learning to rhyme on command under pressure. The longer the incantations and/or the more a rhyme was repeated, the stronger and more complicated the spell could be. But at least if one messed up a magic spell they weren't killed.

"I could've been practicing and working on this on the way here!" Devyn exclaimed.

"You should've made sure it was actually a dragon. Lindworms are so obnoxious to listen to!"

"Yes, I should've double-checked—but how could he not know what a lindworm is? Holy Mother, I hate questers. How did he make it out alive? Holy Mother, Holy Mother, Holy Mother, I can't do this, I can't do this, I can't do this…" Devyn fell to the floor of the inn room, shaking and crying in a loose cross-legged position, one hand on zir head.

"Your poetry isn't that awful. I've heard worse from an earth demon!" Jackie sneered.

"Is that supposed to comfort me? Because it didn't," zie said. "And it's not that… I promised Akácia that I could do this, that I could help her and Kinai's son… I hadn't seen her in ten years *because of you*, Kinai is dead *because of you*, the remaining exorcists don't talk to me *because of you*, because they're terrified of you, Akácia… when she saw me, when she saw *you*, she told me how she remembered it all as if it'd happened yesterday. My best friend barely writes because when she thinks of me, she thinks of *you devouring* Kinai. After *ten years* she finally comes around because she needs my help, *her son* needs my help and —despite all my skill, all my knowledge, all my experience—I can't help. I'm a failure."

"I don't think you're a failure," Lio said, standing at the doorway.

Devyn jumped. "How much of that did you hear?"

"Enough. I'm sorry for telling you it was a dragon. I genuinely thought it was one. Is there anything I can do to help?"

"Uh…" zie thought about it. "Are you any good at poetry?"

"Poetry!?"

"Yes. Lindworms only speak in poetry, and we *have* to do the same. We get one slip-up, and after that the lindworm will eat us."

"Oh! That uh, that is a pretty important distinction. My bad." Lio rubbed the back of his neck sheepishly. "Anything else?"

"We need a new gift, so the lindworm will actually accept our apology. Given the circumstances, I want us to be as polite as possible, and it'll take me a few hours to find what I need. And we both need to sleep."

"Then leave the poetry to me, you fix the gift situation. Will the lindworm accept haikus?"

"Only on a technicality. So yes."

"Then let's get to work. I trust you."

"I don't trust you, but I can't do this alone."

☾

Devyn and Lio approached the lindworm's cave. Autumn vines clung to the rock walls, snow blanketing the area. They arrived at the cave summit, where the red lindworm lay amongst the neatly organized stacks of gifts that ranged from books, dried flowers, to assorted jewelry.

The lindworm saw them approach.

Devyn said,

> "Wise and great lindworm
>
> Of your belongings returned
>
> And gifts for you, too."

The lindworm said,

> "Ah yes, good morning to you all as well
>
> I must admit I recognize not you
>
> But your good tidings cause my heart to swell;
>
> Those who return my belongings are few.
>
> You who speaks to me in haiku I know
>
> The exorcist who trammeled Jakevais.
>
> Do not be surprised, you're known high and low
>
> By many creatures with kindness and vice.
>
> I am the keeper of many things fey,
>
> Treasures with secrets many would have burned.
>
> What is it that you have brought with today?
>
> For curse or enchantment is it returned?
>
> Because of your good heart, selfish or not
>
> Your woes I'll hear, a lesson I hope taught."

Devyn said,

> "Behold this treasure
>
> A medallion of gold
>
> It has cursed my friend."

Lio said,

> "I stole your treasure
>
> Nine moons ago while you slept.
>
> I regret that choice."

Devyn said,

> "On every half-moon
>
> Transformation, like clockwork.
>
> A horrible beast."

Lio said,

> "Each time I suffer
>
> And each time it worsens more.
>
> Nothing has helped me."

Devyn said,

> "The best in the land
>
> We have all tried to help him
>
> But there is nothing."

Lio said,

> "I come to you now
>
> With the treasure that I stole
>
> Asking for your help, please."

The lindworm rumbled. Devyn stared in horror at Lio, who immediately realized his mistake. The lindworm accepted their gifts and the golden box with the medallion, hot smoke oozing out of its nostrils, and said,

"Your grave ailment is familiar.

Gifted to me by a wizard long gone.

'At half-moon rise you will be a monster

With no break from the pain until next dawn.'

Sometimes humans fall for its gilded trap,

Every last one has perished from madness,

And if that doesn't, your soul it will sap.

Of course, I know how to flee this darkness.

The answer that you seek I shall impart:

It is found at the start of this tale

Through fire and suffering of your heart

For then your spirit will cleanse its ail.

There is more to this I could have expressed,

But with haikus I am quite unimpressed."

◗

"But with haikus I am quite unimpressed," Devyn repeated bitterly in a mocking voice. "We only messed up once."

"Lindworms are so annoying," Jackie agreed. **"Real beasts in a scuffle, and pretentious poetry elitists, too!"**

"And what do they mean by 'through fire and suffering of the heart'? I know lindworms must speak in poetry, I get that, but there's *got* to be a less ambiguous statement than that. Which fire? What kind of suffering? What's that bit about 'at the start of this tale'? Gaw!" Devyn was worked up.

Lio had been quiet since leaving the lindworm's cave. He remained quiet the rest of the way.

At the inn Devyn and Lio sat in the tavern below the guest rooms. Lio had a jug of wine.

"The half-moon is in three nights," Devyn said, "I know we just got here, but we have to make as much distance between here and—"

"I'd like to stay another night," Lio interrupted. "It's gonna happen anyways. It's nice here. It's a change of pace."

Taken aback, Devyn took a second to process.

"Okay, we can stay another night. You're right. Besides, I'm sure there's interesting things here. But we do need to leave before the half-moon."

"What does it matter?" Lio asked. "Whether I'm five miles away or fifty, long as I'm not in the city when I transform—"

Devyn shushed him. Zie glanced around the tavern carefully. Lio's eyes were wide, startled. One person glanced over specifically in their direction, but she looked away when zie stared back at her.

"What's the big deal?" Lio asked.

"Some people," Devyn explained in a lowered voice, "like to hunt werefolk."

"But I haven't hurt anyone!" he protested softly.

"That doesn't matter. Monster hunters rarely care about that. You can't just use the T-word in a public place like this." Zie glanced at the woman. "You never know who's listening."

◑

Devyn was on edge after that, keeping a cautious eye on the people around them while Lio enjoyed the city. Nothing happened. Once zie swore that zie saw the tavern woman in the streets, but at a second look she was gone.

Then they left.

Devyn made the executive decision to leave on foot. Aware it would be slower, but zie figured this way there'd be fewer people who knew where zie and Lio were going. Fewer loose ends. They made it seven miles from the city with soft-spoken conversations. Devyn kept an eye on the sky. They stopped at a small clearing for the evening, a spot lightly covered in snow and motley leaves. It was quiet, complete with a sturdy oak for Lio.

"Comfortable?" zie asked.

"As much as I can be."

Sunlight died.

The transformation happened.

Lio cried and shrieked and roared, his body convulsing. His struggles fell on Devyn's steel-clad heart, which remained unmoved. Jackie chattered to him, which wasn't distracting. Zie kept an ear out for trouble, balancing the world and concentrating, meditating near Monster Lio. The golem city was nearby, so zie couldn't risk it.

"Someone else is here."

Devyn opened zir eyes, watching the shadows.

"I know you're there," zie said calmly. "Show yourself."

From the trees, a woman approached with a crossbow.

Devyn grimaced, hating being right.

"What're you doing with this monster?" she asked, wearing a hood. "Why haven't you killed it?"

"Lio hasn't hurt anyone," Devyn said calmly. "He's contained."

"That *thing* is a monster!" she growled. "His very existence is an abomination, a danger to others! He can't be trusted!"

"Lio has not harmed a fly," zie said firmly. "I am quite capable of handling him. Have you come here just to give me your unsolicited two-cents on something that is none of your business?"

She laughed, "no. I'm here to slay a monster."

Devyn leapt to zir feet. She levied her crossbow, a silver arrowhead pointed at Lio.

"Don't!"

The silver-tipped arrow flew!

Devyn tried to shield Lio but was too late. Zir concentration broke! Lio's chains dissipated. He roared, blood oozing from a wound in his arm.

"I missed!"

Before she could reload, Lio berserked and lunged at her!

"Energy!" zie said.

Lio mauled the monster slayer. Zie fired a beam of white light at Lio, knocking him off his feet and sending him running. The hunter lay bleeding out on the ground.

Devyn went over to her.

She coughed up blood. "See? A monster. That's all he is. All he ever will be."

Devyn growled, "I had him under control. *You* didn't listen, *you* broke my focus, *you* provoked him, *your* actions are the reason he's on the loose." Zie stood up.

"I was doing what was right."

"No one asked you."

"Can… can you heal me?" she asked meekly. "Light mage."

Devyn flinched. Zie wanted to find Lio. "I can try something quickly, but I'm not a healer. And I have to stop him from hurting anyone else!" Zie leaned over her and placed one hand on her chest wound and another on the closest tree root.

"Underneath your leaves, before you I kneel

Life drained by us thieves, I need you to heal."

Dim light illuminated the tree and the hunter's wound, the tree wilted as her wound sealed up with scabs. Devyn took zir lantern in hand to see the scope of the damage.

That's a lot of blood. She's not going to make it.

Zie stood up, taking the lantern with zir. "I'm sorry. That's the best I can do."

Devyn ran off in the direction of Lio.

It was hard to miss his path of destruction. In the lantern's light zie saw trampled bushes and blood splattered on the ground.

"That blood smells good," Jackie said.

"Can you tell how far away he is?"

"Just use the All-Seeing-Eye spell, or a tracker."

"You're right." Devyn didn't like doing that if zie could avoid it, but Lio needed to be found *now*. Zie took the blood covered grass, drew a circle and triangle in the mud, placed dried onions in one corner, found specific leaves to put in another, and dried wood ears in the other, and set the blood-grass in the center.

"With blood from my friend, one I need to track,

So, this leaf I send, my friend I want back."

The leaves floated up and glowed red, drifting toward the direction of Lio. One leaf flew away to tag him, the other guided Devyn to him. A bright flash of red in the distance told zir where Lio was.

"From the flash of red my friend has been found,

I don't want more dead; he needs to be bound."

Roaring.

Devyn caught up to Lio, who was bound to the ground under the weight of Devyn's magic chains. He struggled violently. Blood oozed from the wound, the arrow embedded deep into Lio's arm.

"Boy, you're so lucky she missed your heart," Devyn said, exhausted. Zie assessed the damage. "That's a huge arrow. She really came for blood—sorry, Lio, this is gonna hurt." Devyn restrained him tighter with more magic chains, then pulled the arrow out.

Roaring!

Devyn set the arrow down. Fire encompassed zir right hand.

"Cauterize."

Zie stuck three flaming fingers into the wound. Lio roared and struggled in pain. It stopped most of the bleeding.

"He tastes good." Jackie said. *"Tastes like his father."*

"I don't need that type of commentary right now."

"What're you going to do with the hunter?"

"Depends if she's alive when we get back. I don't think that dark magic spell helped. I can't allow her body to be found, and now that I've thought about it, I don't think letting her go free is a wise decision either."

When the morning came Lio couldn't remember anything, let alone why he was in pain *and* had a gaping hole in his arm. Devyn took him back to camp, where the hunter lay cold.

Upon looking at her lifeless body, Lio cried. "I didn't mean to hurt her! I couldn't control myself!"

"I know," Devyn said. "We can't change the past. This is what I was afraid of happening."

"This is all my fault!"

"Lio, you had every right to want to stay another night. You had every right to expect to be left unbothered while I restrained you. As unfortunate as this situation is, my pity is limited. Monster slayers, especially ones like her, have this violent ideology about purity and werewolves. She attacked you with intent to kill, yet you had done nothing wrong except exist."

"I still murdered her!" Lio cried. He fell to the ground. "Devyn, I'm a monster! Is this what my life is going to be like? Pain and murdering people?"

"Probably."

"I don't think I can live like this, Devyn!" Tears streamed from Lio's face.

Devyn sighed, "I understand. Don't worry, I made a promise to your mother—I won't give up on you. If I personally have to restrain you every two weeks until you die of old age, or whatever the lindworm said, then so be it."

"*Devyn*, I'm just going to get worse. There's no treatment for me, and the lindworm says this *will* kill me slowly. I'm just going to be in more pain, I'm going to be harder to restrain. I'm going to hurt more people. I don't want to live like that!"

Zie took a moment to answer, conflicted. "I understand. Your feelings are valid and real and justified. But we haven't figured out what the lindworm meant, and your mom will be so excited to see you. Don't you want to see your mom?"

Lio paused, then nodded, "I want to see my mom."

"Then we're going to go back to the temple."

"What about her?" he gestured to the hunter.

"I didn't forget about her." Devyn opened the lantern wide. "Step back."

Zie breathed in, recollecting the enchantment zie had prepared. Devyn breathed out.

"Death lay before us, she gave quite a chase.

Jakevais, consume her, leave not a trace."

Zie opened the lantern entirely, fire wrapped around zir hand as a great fiery being emerged from the lantern. She stretched.

"Fresh air, sure have missed you!" Jackie said. She stepped toward the body, her infernal body not leaving a cinder on the grass. The primeval being encapsulated the hunter's blood-drained body, incinerating it. When she was done, she said, "thanks for the meal."

Devyn looked at her, saying sternly, "thank you…?" Zie tightened zir will around her, forcing her to her knees.

"Thank you, *Master.*"

"You're welcome," Devyn said, closing the lantern as she was pulled back inside.

Lio said in awe, "that was… horrifying." Devyn stopped Lio from bleeding with an incantation, then wrapped the injury with cloth.

"Sometimes it's necessary. Let's go."

◑

Akácia was waiting for them at the temple.

"Oh, my boy! What happened to your arm?" Akácia asked, embracing Lio. He flinched.

"Sensitive subject," Devyn said, setting zir bag down. "We'll talk to you about it later. Good to see you."

"I missed you, Mom," Lio hugged Akácia tightly. "I'm glad you're back from your trip."

Devyn found the Head Monk and told him the highlights.

"That is troubling news, but I'm glad you were at least able to return that horrid jewel. Any idea what the lindworm meant?"

"Not a clue. I was hoping you might."

"No, but I hope for Lio's sake that you find the answer to this riddle. For now, I shall see to healing his wound."

Lio and Akácia talked in private for a while. Devyn pondered the lindworm's riddle. Suddenly, there was a knock on the door. Akácia.

"Come in," zie said, scribbling out another thought.

"Evening, friend!"

"Evening."

"How are you holding up? I heard you had to use… her."

"Honestly? I feel terrible. I don't care so much that I had to use Jackie like that, it happens, but…" Devyn sighed. "I don't know what I'm supposed to do, Akácia. Lio officially has a body count, *that's a problem*, and honestly, he's really shaken by it. Ever since I took him to see the werewolves, he's been so depressed, and I don't blame him. He's fifteen, turning sixteen tomorrow, and he's in chronic pain and suffering that is only going to get worse and I've tried *everything*—" Devyn shook. "Akácia, I'm supposed to be the best of us, even the lindworm knew me! 'The exorcist who trammeled Jakevais', who bound her, a *primeval spirit*, to *my soul* to save thousands of lives. Sure, my lifespan is now absurdly long, but at the cost of watching all my loved ones *die*. I've mastered light and dark magic, I even have basic fire magic now because of Jackie! I'm the best there is, and I *don't know how to help*. The answer is right in front of me and I don't understand what it means. Lio, he-"

"He wants to die. I know."

Devyn cried, "and I… I don't blame him. I get it. If I were him, I'd want to die, too. He has the *right* to die, but I made a promise to you… I'm sorry, I just don't know what to do except be by his side while he suffers."

Akácia hugged zir.

"Devyn, you're my best friend. In all the years I've known you, your heart has always been in the right place, but you can put aside your feelings and do what needs to be done when the rest of us falter. That's why you were burdened with Jakevais. That's why Kinai died."

"I didn't—"

"Dear, I *know* you. We've known each other for over half our lives. Every time you write you talk about Kinai. I *know* you feel responsible for his death. I *know* that this is more than just about Lio to you, it's about me, it's about Kinai. I *know* how much she wears at you, how her constant presence eats away at you, how lonely you feel because no one else in the world understands the pressure that you feel. I can't even begin to fathom how it feels to have her bound to you. But you're the only one of us who could've survived that ceremony. *That's why* you take on what no one else is willing to do. Kinai couldn't do that. And I've felt responsible for his death, too, all this time. But Devyn, it's been ten years, and you're *not responsible* for his death any more than I am. Yes, I've had to have my space and process, and yes, I've had to do it away from you *because Jakevais terrifies me*, just like I know she terrifies you. But it's been ten years. Kinai is dead, and Lio needs you now. I know you're doing your best now just like you were then. I trust you, Devyn. I trust you to hold fast to what needs to be done, even when the hearts of everyone around you falter and bend. I trust you, Devyn."

◐

They spent several days together as the three of them, being a family. Lio cheered up a bit, but Devyn saw that he still wasn't the same. Not even the love of his mother could help.

After the trip to the lindworm, the monks offered to give Devyn a night off and keep Monster Lio restrained with silver, but Lio wanted zir and Akácia there for comfort and moral support until the transformation was over. On the second floor of the temple, the two laid on the floor catching up as Devyn wrote more of zir entry in the *Big Book of Monster Magic*, including the lindworm's puzzling sonnet. It was maybe an hour after sunset when Devyn felt zir dark magic chains break, then suddenly an explosion shook the temple!

They looked at each other.

"Lio!" Devyn exclaimed, jumping up. They ran down the stairs toward the were-den.

In the basement nine monks lay passed out as the Head Monk fought against three other monks in a battle of light magic—Lio was gone! There was a gaping Monster-Lio-sized-hole leading to the outside world.

"What's going on here?" Devyn asked.

"Where's my son!?" Ruptured silver chains littered the floor.

"These men are traitors! Heretics!" The Head Monk exclaimed before being knocked out by a blast of white energy.

"Energy!" Akácia exclaimed. She blasted the closest one.

Devyn shouted, "why did you set him free?"

The tall one said, "we were trying to kill him, not release him!"

That was all zie needed to hear.

"Energy!" A beam of light magic from both zir

and Akácia.

"How *dare* you attack my son!" Akácia roared. Another energy beam.

"Akácia! I'll fight them off, you go find Lio!"

She nodded, fleeing after her son through the hole.

The shorter rogue monk said, "that monster is a murderer and an abomination! His existence is a disgrace to the sanctity of this temple and puts her Holy Mother to shame!"

Rage burgeoned in zir heart.

"I've had *enough* of people like you," Devyn growled.

Three energy beams, one from each monk.

"Dissipate," zie said.

The monks stared in awe. Devyn took a step forward.

"Velvet Night," zie said. A wave of shrieking purple energy surged out of zir, fueled by zir own sullen memories, sending the rogue monks into a fit of despair.

"How does it feel?" zie asked. "Night Mares."

Horse-headed shadow beasts enshrouded them, feeding on their despair, contorting the rogue monks into writhing agony.

The long-haired one shouted, "Butterfly Cleanse!" White light butterflies ate at the Night Mares. "Felicitous Lepidopterans." They shifted into prismatic rainbow hues, happy memories curing the monks of Devyn's sullen memories.

"Moth Eater." A magic black bat ate the butterflies. "Energy." White light from Devyn's hand, attacking the taller monk. "Light Wave." The three toppled over from the white light pulse.

"Divine Descension!" The long-haired one exclaimed. A massive white pressure forced Devyn to the floor.

"Energy!" Short said.

"Light Wave!" Tall said. Light magic pulsated from him.

"Reflect," zie said, struggling under the weight. Blasts of shattered light scattered across the destroyed were-den. The monks jumped to the sides to escape.

Devyn stood up.

"Velvet Night."

They ran from the shrieking purple wave.

Devyn's will focused, resolve hardened.

"You're not going anywhere."

Chains materialized from the air, ensnaring the ankles of all three of them.

Short chanted,

"From these chains depart, please hold fast and true!

With power of my heart, I release you!"

Tall's magic chains evanesced. Devyn did not allow his escape to distract zir.

The monks writhed.

"Have mercy!" Long-Hair pleaded.

"No."

"For the love of Her Holy Mother, spare us, please!"

Devyn's ironclad heart ignored them.

"Jakevais, I present two apostates.

Philosophies of malice and violence,

Death unto innocents it emanates,

So death unto them will be their silence."

Zie opened the lantern, fire around zir hand, Jakevais emerged. She entombed them, cackling gleefully. Their screams rang in Devyn's ears. They faded. The lantern closed, and she went back inside.

Devyn checked on the Head Monk and the others. All alive. No injuries looked fatal.

Zie said,

"I seek to pry upon where my friend be,

With this All-Seeing-Eye, I wish to see."

A shadowy hole ripped open in front of Devyn, revealing zir intended sight. *There she is.*

Devyn stepped out of the were-den into the forest, following in hot pursuit of zir friends. They were at the village. Zie'd seen flashes of torches in the background, which couldn't mean anything good.

Zie arrived at the village to see Akácia shielding Monster Lio from the weapons of an angry mob.

"Kill the beast!"

"Off with his head!"

"Stab him in the heart!"

Arrows shot at Lio, who berserked on everyone who attacked him, barreling past Akacia, and mauling and goring many as objects deflected off his dragon-scale skin. Two silver arrows jutted out of him.

"Velvet Night," Devyn said, temporarily subduing the mob.

"Devyn, chain Lio!"

"Great idea, and then give the angry mob a defenseless target!"

"Can't you subdue them, then?"

"I am!"

"With chains?"

"No! There's hundreds!"

Tall's voice boomed, "Felicitous Lepidopterans." A kaleidoscope of prismatic butterflies cured the villagers of their despair.

From the top of a building, Tall said, "citizens! Before you is the beast who's been living amongst you, ungrateful of your hospitality. He's killed an innocent woman and now he's attacked many of you tonight. Are you going to let this abomination, this crime against the Holy Mother, go unpunished?"

"No!" Resounded the throngs.

"And are we going to let those two mages stop us?"

"No!"

"Then I say we kill those monster-loving traitors, too, for murdering two brave monks just moments ago!"

Devyn and Akácia stood back to back. Lio was allowed to flee.

"They're letting the monster escape!"

"Kill the monster-lovers!"

Akácia fired energy beams at Tall, and Devyn materialized Moth Eaters, Velvet Nights, Night Mares, Shields, and more quick attacks that would not kill, both trying to deflect and evade countless projectiles.

"Soul Pulse!" Devyn said, forcing out brute strength soul energy into a palm strike, pushing back several torch, pitchfork, and spear wielders.

"Shield!" Akácia exclaimed.

"Darkness Ascent." Purple magic lifted the crowd off their feet and dropped them from five feet, hurting and knocking them off-balance.

"Light Wave! Shield!"

"Velvet Night!"

"Divine Descension!"

"Shield!"

"Shield!"

"Energy!"

"Morning Star!" Akácia blinded the mob with a giant orb of light magic. It exploded, hitting villagers.

"Where'd the monk go?" Devyn asked.

"I lost track of him! He's probably after Lio!"

"Bastion!" A light magic dome now protected them from attacks, and no attacks could get out. Devyn took Akácia's hand. "Together."

Zie whispered the spell to her, one they'd made together as apprentices. The bastion spell would only last a short period. Long enough to cast real magic.

She nodded.

Together they shouted, "By our plight we beseech to you our woes

Because of our fight, we must now impose:

Take this light unto you, our hateful foes,

Blinded in sight you shall receive this rose."

Radiant wild roses grew from the ground, glittering pearlescent beauties that glowed and trapped every person in the crowd in thorns. Arms and feet were tangled in rose vines, and each person's eyes were covered perfectly in the glittering pearlescent roses.

"I love that spell," Devyn said. Cries of pain from the mob filled the air.

"Lio!" Akácia exclaimed, running off.

"I think I know where he is!" Zie ran with her. "Follow me!"

They ran through the woods, the way becoming increasingly familiar until zie heard roaring and howling. In a clearing in the woods, a werewolf patrol and Monster Lio fought against Tall, who was easily holding his own.

"Energy!" Devyn and Akácia said simultaneously. Two light beams struck Tall and knocked him over.

Tall lashed out with a series of light waves.

"Enough of this!" Devyn bellowed. Magical chains gripped Tall's legs, forcing him to kneel, his hands binding, too. Lio fled again. Akácia and the werewolves ran after him.

"You're making a grave mistake letting these monsters live. He's only going to hurt more people!"

"Lio hadn't hurt a fly until people like you came along."

"He murdered an innocent woman! You were there!"

"Yes, I was there. I know what happened more than you or anyone else alive possibly could."

"Monster-lover! Quit wasting your time on them! You should be using your talents to help people, not monsters!"

"I *am* helping people."

Devyn opened zir lantern.

"What—what are you doing?"

"Letting you join your friends."

"No—please! You're making a mistake!"

Zie repeated from before, "Jakevais, I present an apostate.

Philosophies of malice and violence,

Death to innocents it does emanate,

So death unto him will be his silence."

Fire. Screaming. Devyn watched him burn with a cold gaze. Zie didn't put her back.

"Aren't I done?" Jackie asked, perplexed.

"Not yet." *I don't understand the lindworm. But I understand what I have to do.*

Devyn and Jackie followed the night trail deeper into the woods. Lio was rampaging, Akácia and the werewolves were trying to stop him. Zie focused intently on Lio, who now had six silver arrows in him. Dark magic chains wrapped around him.

"Devyn!" Akácia exclaimed. She froze. "Why is she out?"

"Because I told her to be."

Zie saw her pause. A look of what might have been understanding settled across her face.

"At least take the arrows out?"

"No point. He'll just hurt more. I'm sorry, Akácia."

She looked away from Devyn. "I trust you. I'll tell the others to move back." She and the werewolves went several yards deeper into the forest.

Devyn approached the struggling Lio, who gazed up at Devyn in pain.

"Lio, I'm sorry. I should've done this sooner. For your sake." Devyn breathed in, resolve holding steadfast.

"Jackie. Devour him. Engulf in flame,

'Through fire and suffering of the heart':

No more of this painful life, no more blame.

I've done all that I can. I've played my part."

Devyn looked away as Jakevais cackled and devoured Lio. Her flames ate at his monstrous flesh, incinerating him slowly as the boy shrieked and roared. Kinai's screams rang in Devyn's ears.

When it was all over, zie closed the lantern, and collapsed to the ground. Tears poured down zir face, zir body exhausted and worn. Zie felt Akácia embrace zir in the darkness. She was crying, too.

"I'm sorry, Akácia. I failed you."

"You didn't fail me."

"How? I just killed you and Kinai's son."

She hugged Devyn. "I asked you to end my son's suffering. And you did. I knew when I asked you months ago that this was a possibility."

"Then why ask me?" zie asked, shaking.

"Because I trust you to do what needs to be done. You did right by Lio, so you did right by me."

"If we'd just—"

"You're not a failure, Devyn."

"But the lindworm!"

She clung to zir, crying, embracing zir. "You're not a failure. You helped my son when everyone else gave up on him. I trust you."

Together, they cried under the trees well into the morning light.

About the Author

Burgundy Pendragon has a Bachelor of Science in Biology (Ecology & Organismal Studies), Environmental Studies (Science Track), and English, with a minor in Creative Writing and the LGBTQ+ Studies Certificate. They are proud to call themselves a queer, Jewish, non-binary, autistic, ADHDer, with a fervent love for ecology, fantasy, animals, Pokémon, world-building, literature, audiobooks, and poetry. They studied at the University of Wisconsin Oshkosh.

Pendragon uses three pronoun sets: they/them/theirs, zie/zir/zirs, and vi/vir/virs, in ascending order of preference. Feel free to use any of these three sets when referring to vir.

LANTERN is Pendragon's first published book, courtesy of Bull & Dragon Press LLC.

About LANTERN

I wrote LANTERN in the Spring of 2018, the semester immediately following my return from my three-month stay at the Taylor Wilderness Research Station in Idaho's incomparable Frank Church–River of No Return Wilderness. I was inspired both by a character I had created while out there, whom I played as when playing imagination with the local ten-year-old, and by the works of medieval writers in my Chaucer And His Age class. This would be one of two medieval literature courses I would take with the same professor, Dr. Boehler. I must apologize to him because while I *was* listening, I was inspired not to take any amount of diligent notes, but to write this story instead. And I thank him, for being willing to read the unrevised version of LANTERN all those years ago.

These medieval inspirations show up in my desire to incorporate poetry, and for the book to look the way that it does. Devyn's name comes from the word "devyn" in a Chaucer text, which I had originally mistranslated in my head to be an older spelling of "divine" and thus pronounced "deh-veen." I found out later, that it is an older spelling of the name "Devin" and it means "soothsayer," which is thematically appropriate, too. Additionally, Devyn uses the pronouns zie/zir/zirs because I like the way that set sounds and it felt strange and magical enough to fit the strange and magical Devyn. Any similarities to a friend that I may have, is truly and sincerely, entirely coincidental. I swear.

Further, as much as I love world-building and beautiful prose in my fantasy, I decided to try something different with LANTERN. I chose to take a minimalist approach to world-building and descriptions. I feel this was done to great effect, but of course, there is always a different moment where everyone tells me they'd wished there'd been just a little bit more description. I want the appearance of the characters and the setting to be left to interpretation—perhaps the "forest" is a Siberian taiga, or an equatorial jungle a la South America or Africa—it doesn't really matter, and I think there is actually something magical about the fluidity of Devyn's world, with just enough concrete details to anchor it and give it life.

Lastly, I want it known that Devyn is in fact meant to be autistic and non-binary, just like me.

Acknowledgements

I would like to take time to thank the people who read my early drafts of LANTERN and supported me: Dr. Boehler, Dr. Cannon, my friends Jon and Danielle, my mother, and of course, my best friend and partner, Benjamin. Special thanks to Danielle for being the critical eye that I needed and inadvertently line-editing my manuscript. And of course, to my best friend Shaii, for being amazing and turning my manuscript into a book, and to Aaron, for making the absolutely gorgeous cover art.

Sneak Peak of
The Existentialist Dread of a Gen Z'er

Putting Out the Stars

Harvesting stars wasn't anything new to us. It was a long, complicated process with a lot of paperwork and a lot of scientific testing that the Intergalactic Federation of Humans mandated before we could even begin allowing halos to move in, or mining operations to start, let alone the final act of putting up the miles-long panels that would wrap around the system's star.

The Distant Yearning for Stars from Other Nebulae (D.Y.S.O.N.) program was in charge of testing and approving mining on each individual planet or moon. Asteroid belts were free game, of course. Our primary objective was to find any traces of life, and if we did, the local star would not be harvested for its energy in order to preserve the life that was found around it. Extraterrestrial life was rare but not unheard of in the Milky Way Galaxy. I was an astrobiologist from a halo colony in the Kuiper belt. I took my work seriously and with great pride, and as much as I always wanted to go on an adventure exploring alien worlds with alien ecosystems, I had three kids to take care of, one of each. So I took a job as an astrobiologist for D.Y.S.O.N., the program that paves the way for humanity through the ever-growing expanses of space. It was worthwhile work, but sending probes and looking at data sheets got old, even in the cosmos.

This particular star, a single G-type main sequence with four rocky planets and one gas giant, was in the final stages of being approved for large scale mining and light harvesting operations. Civilian halos only moved into some star systems, and this wasn't going to be one of them for reasons only the higher-ups understood. The root of my confusion came from the fact that these are the sorts of stars halo colonies were usually built around. G-type main sequence stars are, after all, the same type of star that our species evolved around an eon ago, the Sun.

"Sir," I asked the branch chief, "this is a G-type star, why are we making plans for harvesting when we could be building halo colonies?"

"Admins want to harvest the sunlight from this star instead, something about the panels being more efficient with G-types and getting hundreds of more teragrams of fuel," she said.

I gave her an uncertain look.

"Karl, just get back to work. It's none of your business, anyways."

I sighed. I knew why we were pushing for more fuel; it was so we could finally make the push to send manned expeditions to the Andromeda Galaxy. A major leap for humanity, reaching beyond our galaxy into the next. But it was an expensive endeavor.

The datasheets in front of me started to blur together. I couldn't concentrate anymore. I signed out and took a lunch break in the breakroom. I wondered about my children—*how are they doing right now?* I glanced up to stare out the window at the burning ball of plasma burning a quarter of a lightyear away. It reminded me of home. Almost. Except the Sun from the Kuiper Belt was distant and cold, even as a red giant. *Is this what the Sun used to look like?* I imagined what it would be like to step onto the shores of a sandy beach with my children, a moon tugging on the water, feeling the warmth of a star on my skin, and hearing the squeals of my children running around on a breathable planet. Of course, I had no idea what any of this was like, only images and videos I'd seen growing up in the Kuiper Belt, but I yearned to know what humanity once knew.

Tired and exhausted, I sat back down at my desk and stared at the datasheets more. I noticed a new file from our latest and final probe, the Alpha-9-Orion Arm-CMVIII. The probe had been sent to explore the watery moon of the local gas giant.

The numbers were boring me. It was difficult to concentrate. I tried reminding myself that I was doing this for the kids, so they could have a good life with the best education I could get them by being on this small research-based halo. But that required that I kept working for D.Y.S.O.N., no matter how tedious the datasheets became.

I sifted through the pictures the probe took. High quality images of the surface water were coming through. I shook my head. *Water should've put this moon at the top of the priority list. Administration doesn't know what they're doing anymore.*

An image caught my eye. "What is *that?*" I perked up in my seat. I opened up another image beside it, and another, and another, and another, and they all showed the same thing. I checked the next datasheet, and in my excitement I could see the patterns in the numbers, all of them confirming what the images showed: *multi-cellular life!*

I called up the branch chief, "sir, you've gotta come see this! There's life!"

The branch chief was at my office in a minute sharp.

"Show me," she said sternly. I was put off by her annoyance, when I was expecting enthusiasm.

"Check it out," I said eagerly. "Microscopic multi-cellular life! This is amazing!" I grinned at her.

"This is incredible," she said, "but I'm going to need you to delete this."

"… what?"

"You heard me."

"Yes, sir, but I don't understand."

"I'm saying, that if you don't delete this data, and anymore that comes in about this, then I *will* terminate you."

I stared at her, incredulous. "Sir, this is *life* that we found."

"I understand that, and I won't say this again: if you don't delete this data *and* pretend this never happened, then I'm going to terminate your employment."

"I… I understand, sir."

I didn't understand. I gazed at the images in front of me. I thought about my children. I cried at my desk. I don't know how long I sat there and cried, but it was a while. Eventually, I made my decision. Knowing that their sun was going to be harvested without it, I deleted the data.

Grab-N-Guilt

I stare at the bottled tea options before me in the Kwik Trip cooler. An internet joke, *when Wisconsinites die, we just respawn at the last Kwik Trip we were at*, runs through my head, and I giggle. I weigh my options. Plastic is cheaper, but glass doesn't lose quality in the recycling process, but plastic doesn't sit in landfills like a rock, but glass is easier to reuse and doesn't contaminate drinks with hydrocarbons that act as pseudo-estrogens. I decide on glass. I try to find one that's Rainforest Alliance Certified, but this location only has USDA Certified Organic—a label I know doesn't mean much, but I figure it's better than nothing. Of course, I could always *not* buy bottled tea, but I'm on a road trip to Chicago, and it's hot, and I like the taste. I pick out some beef jerky, too, my classmates' presentations on animal cruelty and concentrated animal feedlot operations flash through my mind, and I feel a moment of guilt before I grab the chewy snack. I don't have to look to know that there's no "grass-fed beef jerky" option at the gas station. I hold out my two snacks, satisfied and excited with my acquisitions, and I think of all the fossil fuels used to create the plastic, mold the glass, ship the food, and transport the snacks across the country from the factories they came from. I think of the slave-labor that almost certainly went into the tea-harvesting of my drink, or the cane sugar plantations, or the rainforest trees slashed and burned to make way for the cattle that is now my jerky. I put the snacks on the counter and pay. I return to the car, where my friend is waiting for me after filling the car with gasoline. And again, I think of all the carbon dioxide and methane that was pumped or burped into the atmosphere just to get me my cheap gas station snacks. I think about the greenhouse effect created by carbon dioxide, how we're long past the point of no return and the Earth's global temperatures are continuing to rise. I eat them happily, guilt plaguing my heart. The worst part, I know, is that even if I hadn't purchased them, even if nobody purchased them ever again, it still wouldn't be enough to make a difference. I think about how our world as we know it will die anti-climatically from the rising ocean levels already slowly drowning island nations, to the extended droughts and heatwaves already destroying crops in Southwest Asia, to the polar vortexes breaking away from the North pole and reaching as far South as Chicago and making the Midwest the coldest place on Earth for a couple days every few winters. I know my attempts to purchase marginally better cheap gas station snacks is fruitless, that even if my friend *could* afford an electric or hybrid car powered by wind and solar energy, even if *everyone* with a car could afford it and we had the infrastructure to support it, none of it would be enough, because it's already too late. So I happily eat my cheap gas station snacks as my friend and I road trip down to Chicago.

Core

When the Next Ones look at our Earth's cores

hundreds or thousands or millions of years into the future,

what will they say about what they see?

       "This spike in Cesium, it is quite peculiar

            What catastrophe happened here?"

Strange patches of motley plastics

      polyurethanes, foam, polyester, polyvinyl chloride,

nylon, polyethylene terephthalate, polycarbonate.

Their archaeologists will find concrete and asphalts,

steel beams and bricks, pockets of rare earth metals

Their paleontologists will see the swaths of corn,

      soybeans and wheat, rice and potatoes

No more large mammals or giant birds.

The glaciologists will see a sudden and unnatural spike

in carbon dioxide and methane.

And they'll see millions and billions of our graves

find a species so prolific, so successful

they're found everywhere,

who had a great and awe-inspiring civilization.

"But what happened to them?

These cores tell so much, they tell us the how, but they don't tell us the why?

And it's hard to fathom why."

Preview of *Parallel Journeys*

Jaqqiq is a Yerazian man from the mountains, conscripted and pulled from his home and the only life he's ever known to fight in a war that isn't his. He leaves behind a dying brother and a heartbroken community, who know that the triannual draft lottery is nothing but a death sentence for their young folks. He goes through basic training, where he deals with giant fae, the terrible combination of his illiteracy and dyslexia, prejudice, and the moralities of war. He works hard to secure himself one of the safer positions in the military, and he gets exactly what he wanted—but why does he feel so guilty? Jaqqiq got what he wanted, and he finds himself unhappy with his choices, and he's forced to grapple with his true feelings about his place in the war that isn't his.

Ashspell is a Ryconan woman from the well-fortified city of Usÿn-don, who had her life planned for her since birth until her family perished in a fire that left her orphaned, to be cared for by her future in-laws. She loves her best friends dearly, the family that she made for herself, which include: a red-eyed mage who acts as everyone's older brother, a charming lockpick from Yerazia, her fiancé since childhood, and her college study-buddy, Torfié. All she wants is to be able to go on adventures with her best friends, to spend her years with them, to be free, but she knows this a dream she cannot have as the weight of socie-tal expectations, her family's legacy, and Torfié's untimely murder make these dreams an impossibility far out of reach for her. In light of her best friend's death, she takes it upon herself to uncover the truth, but her actions have far-reaching consequences for her, and she's forced to deal with her own suppressed feelings in an inescapable hellscape.

Please Follow the Author at:

Twitter: @ dragonkeeper22

To discover more works by Burgundy Athena Pendragon, visit their website at BurgundyPendragon.gay or visit the Bull & Dragon Press website at BullAndDragonPress.com

And if you would like to stay updated on future releases, remember to subscribe to the Bull & Dragon Press Newsletter located at both of these websites!

For fan work:

Tumblr: @ PokemonBiologyIRLtheTabletop

9 781961 603004